THE TERROR OF
BLACK EAGLE TAVERN

Darby Creek
A division of Lerner Publishing Group, Inc.
241 First Avenue North
Minneapolis, MN 55401 U.S.A.

Website address: www.lernerbooks.com

Cover and interior photographs © RDImages/Epics/
Getty Images (tavern); © iStockphoto.com/appletat
(silhouette).

Main body text set in Janson Text LT Std 12/17.5.
Typeface provided by Adobe Systems.

Library of Congress
Cataloging-in-Publication Data

Atwood, Megan.
    The terror of Black Eagle Tavern / by Megan
Atwood.
        p.   cm. — (The paranormalists ; case #02)
    Summary: Todd, a quarterback and popular
senior, asks Jinx and Jackson to investigate a
haunting at his family's tavern, where glasses move
on their own and voices whisper horrible things
each time Todd and his brother are fighting.
    ISBN 978–0–7613–8333–8 (lib. bdg. : alk.
paper)
    [1. Haunted places—Fiction. 2. Taverns
(Inns)—Fiction. 3. Supernatural—Fiction.
4. Brothers—Fiction. 5. Drug abuse—Fiction.
6. Best friends—Fiction. 7. Friendship—Fiction.]
I. Title.
PZ7.A8952Ter 2012
[Fic]—dc23   2011046443

Manufactured in the United States of America
1 – PP –7/15/12

THE PARANORMALISTS
CASE #2

THE TERROR OF
BLACK EAGLE TAVERN

MEGAN ATWOOD

THE PARANORMALISTS

Paranormalists Blog—
INVESTIGATION #01:
FALCON'S PERCH APARTMENTS

Time for an update, Paranormalist Fans. Our first official case turned out to be a bleep-storm. A quick recap of what the investigation team did at Falcon's Perch Apartments:

Subject came to us and said her apartment was trying to kill her. Subject displayed cuts and bruises, complained of disembodied voices, and talked of objects moving of their own accord. In other words, subject had a crapload of paranormal activity to report.

Enter us, the investigation team. We stayed one night, equipped with both the EVP and EMF meters. Also, a stealth cam was set up—and thank goodness, because what came back on video was evidence of a HOAX! That's right, subject tried to fool the investigation team using the familiar look-over-here-while-subject's-partner-in-crime-perpetrates-the-hoax routine. Needless to say, we were disappointed by the outcome.

But I wasn't surprised. This is a tricky business, and people will try to fool you.

The story doesn't end there, though. Oh no. Although the subject's paranormal dilemma did prove to be a hoax, something much more interesting turned up on the EVP. And both yours truly and the other investigator felt a for-real temperature drop! The EMF showed activity, too. So although hoaxers will hoax, it turns out the Falcon's Perch Apartment building DOES have some paranormal activity.

The Rundown on Falcon's Perch Apartment 101 (hoax data discounted)

Electronic Voice Phenomena: Voices detected, said "GET OUT"

Electromotive Force: Slight activity, movement on the meter

Stealth Cam Activity: Nothing

Temperature Fluctuations: Dropped 10 degrees

Verdict: HAUNTED

So, on to our next adventure, PFs! What do you think the otherworld has in store for us? Comments welcome below, and as always, remember that the Paranormalists "SEEK THE TRUTH AND FIND THE CAUSE!"

–Jinx

CHAPTER 1

Whomp! Jackson's body hit the ground, the fall knocking the breath right out of his lungs. He felt person after person pile on top of him. For a second, he panicked. Every part of him was pinned down. He couldn't breathe.

And then, little by little, sun began to shine through his teammates' legs as they got off of him.

Free, he jumped up while Coach yelled, "Showers!" The other members of the football team took off their helmets. Jackson joined the line jogging to the locker room, shuffling his legs to get the tingles out.

Todd McElvoy, the starting quarterback, slapped him on the back as the scents of the locker room wafted their way. *The smell of hard work*, Jackson thought.

Todd said, "Hey, nice catch there. My aim was a little off."

A little off? Jackson thought. The pass almost had him backflipping through the air. And it wasn't Todd's only misfire. He had overthrown or underthrown his passes all practice.

"No worries. I caught it," Jackson replied. He took off his heavy shoulder pads and threw them in his locker, followed by his soaked undershirt. After a beat, he asked, "Everything OK, man?"

Todd closed his locker and leaned against it, still in his practice pants. He seemed to be debating something in his head.

Jackson didn't push as he got dressed. He'd shower at his house—he wanted to get home and make dinner for his mom. He knew it would be a hard day for her: the date of her wedding anniversary. He got sad just thinking about it. After all this time, he still missed his dad so much. And so did his mom, he knew.

Todd seemed to snap out of his trance and said, "Yeah, I'm OK."

Jackson shrugged. "Everyone has an off day. Tomorrow's gonna be better."

Todd nodded and turned away.

Jackson grabbed his bag and began walking to his car, thinking about the type of food he'd prepare. Maybe steak? His mom loved a good steak. He would normally ask Jinx, since she knew his mom about as well as he did, but he was still mad at her from their last fight. He'd figure it out. Jinx could hang out by herself.

A pang ran through him. He didn't want to admit it, but he missed his friend. After two weeks of not hanging out, Jackson felt like he was missing an arm.

He reached his car and had just stuck his keys in the door of the old Chevy Impala when Todd ran up to him.

Jackson looked up in surprise. "Hey. What's up?"

Todd jangled his keys and was quiet for a second. "So, you do, like . . . that website with that one weird girl, right?"

Jackson's expression immediately hardened. He knew Todd was a nice guy, but he was clearly not very tactful. "You mean Jinx."

Todd blushed. "Yeah, sorry. I know you're good friends."

Jackson shrugged and didn't say anything.

Todd went on and stammered, "It's just . . . I think . . . I may have something for you guys to . . . We're having problems . . ."

His face went pale, and Jackson relaxed a little bit. He noticed for the first time the dark circles under Todd's eyes and the trembling of his hands. No wonder he couldn't throw straight.

"What's up, Todd?" He leaned in and whispered, "Do you have a ghost or something?"

Todd looked up and let out a shaky laugh. "It feels so stupid to say out loud. But . . . yeah. I think we're being haunted."

"At your house? What's happening?"

Todd shook his head. "No, at my parents' bar, the Black Eagle Tavern. It's driving customers away." He glanced away and said, so softly Jackson could barely hear him, "We're almost broke."

Jackson nodded. "Well, you came to the right person," he said, unlocking his car door. "We'll see if we can't get rid of your ghosts. I'll call later."

Jackson saw the relief wash over Todd's face as he drove away, and for the first time in a couple weeks, he felt great.

CHAPTER 2

The whole car ride home, Jackson thought about how he'd get Jinx on board. First, he'd have to bridge the huge two-week gap during which he hadn't been talking to her. And he knew that wouldn't be easy—she wasn't the forgiving type. Even though she'd been the one in the wrong. During their last paranormal investigation, she'd hidden a camera without telling Jackson, after he'd explicitly asked her to trust him. Trust wasn't Jinx's strong suit, but still, Jackson had thought she'd at least do him the one favor. She didn't, and Jackson had decided he needed to think for a while.

Shaking his head, he tried to put Jinx and Todd out of his mind. Tonight was his mom's night. She needed to be distracted—then he'd worry about talking to Jinx, getting her to help Todd, and banishing ghosts. Tonight was about steak.

When he got to his house, he found he couldn't park in the driveway—two cars blocked the way. He smiled huge—Grant and Hamilton were home. They knew about the anniversary too, and they must have come home from college to distract his mom. For all the times they'd given him a noogie or a snakebite, they were pretty OK brothers.

After parking, he opened the front door to the most wonderful smell ever. Meat cooking. Something with bacon. And he was pretty sure he detected potatoes.

With the smile still on his face, he turned the corner and walked into the kitchen to find his brothers slaving over dinner. Grant stood by the stove, stirring gravy, while Hamilton sliced bread on the kitchen counter.

But Jackson's eyes were drawn to the girl with the pink-tipped bleached-blonde hair sitting on the counter by the refrigerator. She chewed on a Twizzler and then pointed it at Hamilton.

"You know, if you cut that diagonally, it can hold more butter," she said to him.

Without saying a word, Hamilton turned on the water in the sink, wet his fingers, and flicked the water at the girl.

"Jinx," he said good-naturedly, "if you want to cut the bread, then get your butt over here and do it. Or make yourself useful some other way. Like putting the salad together." Hamilton turned to Jackson. "She's like a cat. You just need to throw some water at her and she'll behave." Then he ducked as a refrigerator magnet flew at his head.

Jackson couldn't help himself—he smiled broadly at her. Jinx smiled back and walked over to him. "So . . . we're good?"

Jackson nodded. Nothing could have touched his heart more than to see everyone rallying to help his mom. He should have known that no matter how mad the two of them got at each other, Jinx would never miss this day. She was family, plain and simple.

"Good. Because we need to get another case going. If we want actual followers, we should have some more actual cases. My last blog post got a hundred hits. We need to keep that going."

Jackson started, "Funny you should say that . . ."

He was cut off by the sound of the front door opening. "Well, holy schmolies!" his mom called out. "The smell in here is to die for!"

She walked into the kitchen, and Jackson saw her eyes moisten. "The gang's all here," she said lightly, then looked away and wiped her eyes. Turning around, she hugged every one of them. Jackson hugged her back extra hard.

She patted his back and then looked around. "When do we get to eat?"

The next day, Jinx and Jackson were in their usual haunt, sitting in Jinx's basement and watching *Ghost Hunters*.

Jackson started, "So, we need an actual case, right?"

Jinx nodded distractedly as she checked her EVP equipment for the thousandth time. Jackson thought she was a little obsessed. Then again, he wanted to bring his dead father back as a ghost, so who was he to talk?

Jinx said, "Yeah, I've been researching haunted places in Portland and—"

Jackson cut her off. "I have one."

Jinx looked at him like he was crazy. "You have a Portland?"

"I have a *case*."

Her eyes narrowed. Jackson knew she was wondering if it was a classmate. She owed him one, though, so maybe she'd go for it. Except for the fact that she hated every single classmate except for him. He steeled himself for the fight.

"Todd McElvoy—"

"No." Jinx cut him off and looked back down at her equipment.

"You didn't even let me say anything!"

"You've said enough. I'm not helping that Neanderthal."

Jackson sighed. "You don't even know him. He's a pretty nice guy."

She looked up from her equipment. "Really. Does he know my name?"

Jackson thought about their conversation earlier. Saying "that weird girl" was *like* knowing her name, right?

He cleared his throat. "Yes! And he even asked for you."

Jinx went back to her equipment. "You're the worst liar. Never play poker, Jackson. Your left eyebrow twitches when you lie."

His arm shot up to his eyebrow. He massaged it and went for the truth. "Well, he called you 'that weird girl.'"

Jackson watched the subtle shift in her posture. She loved being the "weird" one at school. Most people meant it as an insult, but he knew Jinx thought it was great. Anything to get her out of the hole of nobodysville that she'd been stuck in in middle school. The minute she'd started the Paranormalists website, plain Jane was banished and Jinx was born. And she'd loved the notoriety ever since. In fact, Jackson thought she was a little addicted to it.

She raised her eyebrows, "Well, what is this case?"

Jackson smiled to himself and went on. "Evidently, his parents' bar is haunted."

"Haunted how?"

Jackson shrugged. "I don't know, we didn't get that far. We need to meet with him and talk."

"His parents' bar doesn't happen to be the Black Eagle Tavern, does it?"

"Yeah, why?"

Jinx's eyes sparkled. Jackson loved the look she got right before a case. "Because that bar's come up in my research. There are tons of reports of weird things happening there."

Jackson breathed out. "Wow. Well, Todd says there are, too. And it's driving people away. We should meet with him Monday and ask what's going on."

Jinx grinned. "For once, Jackson, I totally agree. Let's hear what he has to say. Even

Neanderthals can be haunted."

Jackson sighed. It was the best he could hope for. "Tomorrow, then."

Jinx took out a Twizzler and snapped off the end with her teeth. "Tomorrow."

CHAPTER 3

Jinx ran a hand through her short, blonde hair and felt for any flyaways. Then she slammed her hand on the picnic table outside the school cafeteria in frustration. She shouldn't care what Todd McElvoy thought, even if she couldn't deny he was pretty good-looking. Still, it wouldn't do for Jackson to see her primping or for Todd to think he was any more of a gift to girls than he already did. Neanderthal. She ruffled her hair until it stood straight up.

Jackson opened the door from the cafeteria, munching on trail mix. With a full mouth he said, "Your hair's sticking up." He dropped down beside her, and Jinx felt the whole table move.

"Yeah, well you've got chocolate on your nose." He didn't, but Jinx couldn't help herself.

Jackson rubbed his nose furiously. "Did I get it?" he asked. Jinx stifled a giggle and shook her head. Jackson rubbed some more until his nose was bright red. "You got it now." She smiled big.

"What?" he asked between munches.

"Nothing." She adored the boy, but he could be too trusting sometimes.

Just then, Todd walked through the cafeteria door, backpack slung over his varsity jacket. His dark hair was tousled, and she could see his magnetic brown eyes from the picnic table. Jinx's hand flew up of its own accord and smoothed her hair again. Jackson gave her a funny look until she rearranged her face to look mean. Todd headed toward the table, his steps hesitant.

Jackson swallowed the rest of his trail mix, then flashed Todd a welcoming smile. "Sit down, man," he said. Todd put his backpack on the table and sat across from Jinx. His eyes met hers for a minute, and she narrowed them. Better for him to think she hated him than to know she thought he was cute.

"Hey, man," Todd said. "Hey, Jinx."

Jinx didn't waste any time. "So you say your parents' bar is haunted. Why should we believe you?"

Jackson's foot connected with her shin, and she yelped. She glared at him, and he glared back.

"We had a little bit of a problem in our last case with our client lying to us," he said to Todd.

Todd nodded. "Travis told me about that afterwards."

Jinx rolled her eyes. Of course he did. Their type knew everything about each other because they were all pretty much the same person. Jocks were like an evil coral reef. "Did he tell you that our fee is five hundred dollars?"

Jackson's head whiplashed toward her. She continued. "If you have a problem with that much, talk to Emily and Travis—our time is valuable, and we have to protect against hoaxers."

"Where am I supposed to get that kind of money?"

Jinx snorted. "Oh come on. Like you're not rich."

Jackson shook his head, and Todd let out a loud bark of a laugh. "I wish. I need these hauntings to stop because I have to get a football scholarship in order to go to college. We're *not* rich—my parents can barely afford to keep the bar running!" He flushed a bright red. Jinx squirmed in her seat. She'd just assumed that because he was good-looking and popular, he was rich, too. She didn't wear guilt very well, so she changed the subject fast.

Jinx cleared her throat and said, more harshly than she meant to, "Just tell us what's happening, and maybe we can figure something out." An idea popped into her head. "If you'll give us a testimonial. And even record a video for our website!"

A ray of hope seemed to light Todd's face. "Yes! I'll totally do those things." He straightened his shoulders. "Well, it all started when . . ." Suddenly a horn sounded from the parking lot to their right.

Even from the picnic table, Jinx could see that the driver looked like Todd. Only a pale and skinny Todd. The driver had dark circles under his eyes, and his fingers drummed on the steering wheel, a steady, frantic beat.

Todd's face darkened. "Just a minute. I'll be right back." He jogged to the car and leaned his head through the window.

Jackson and Jinx looked at each other. "Is that his brother or something?" Jinx asked.

Jackson shrugged. "It looks like it, doesn't it?"

Jinx let out a long, slow whistle. "I bet that dude is strung out."

Jackson laughed. "And how would you know what that looks like?"

"I've seen *CSI*!"

Todd came jogging back to the table, and Jinx and Jackson stopped talking immediately.

He sat down with a thump, and his eyes remained dark.

"That was my brother," Todd mumbled. "He needed to borrow some money." Under his breath he whispered, "Again."

Jinx tilted her head knowingly at Jackson.

"I was just about to say," Todd continued, "that all the stuff in the bar started happening when my brother moved back in and started helping out again. He's twenty, so he'd had his own place for a while, but he had to come live with my parents because of money." His voice drifted off, and he stared into space.

If Jinx didn't watch it, she'd start feeling bad for him. He looked genuinely lost.

"What sorts of things started happening?"

Todd ran a hand through his hair. Jinx pictured running her own hand through his hair, but stopped herself mid-thought. This was business. With a Neanderthal.

He went on, "Well, it didn't happen *right* away. But pretty close to when he came back. Anyway, about two weeks ago when Devon— that's my brother—and I were closing up the bar, things just started . . . moving."

Jinx's eyebrows rose. "Moving how?"

"The glasses on the bar started shaking. At first I thought it was an earthquake, because they were all knocking against each other like the floor was shaking. The liquor bottles started shaking, too."

"How do you know it wasn't just some heavy machinery outside or something like that?" Jinx asked

Todd shook his head. "It was two thirty a.m., after the last bar patron had left. And also, the next thing that happened convinced me . . ." His eyes went dark again.

Jackson leaned forward, and Jinx could feel the whole picnic table shift with him. "What happened?"

"Three glasses came shooting off the bar and crashed into the wall behind us," Todd said. "That's when me and Devon took off. We ran out into the street and just stared at the bar. There wasn't one other person in sight. It couldn't have been anything except . . . well, you know."

Jinx twisted her lip. That did sound pretty convincing. But so had Emily's story, and she had been lying to them. Still, Todd looked completely sincere—just the right amount of upset.

"Were there any other unusual things that happened before that? Any events leading up to it? Or, in years past, have things happened that seemed . . . paranormal?" Jinx had a hard time not adding, "Please." She wanted her research to pan out.

Todd squirmed at the table. "Well, my parents have always said the place was haunted." He ran his hand through his hair again. "In fact, they both talk to the ghosts. Have ever since they bought it in the eighties. They say it keeps the spirits happy and not in haunting mode. And anyway, our ghost is supposed to be, well . . . really nice. Everyone in the neighborhood knows about him. Our ghost, that is." He smiled sheepishly, and Jinx tried really hard not to smile back.

She twisted her lip again. "OK, so it started when your brother came . . . do your parents know that things have been escalating?"

Todd nodded vigorously. "Oh yeah. Everyone knows. We're losing some of our regulars because of this. Like this one guy, Pete, was taking a"—he looked at Jinx and then corrected himself—"going to the bathroom, and all the faucets turned on at once. But worse . . . one of the toilets shot water straight up in the air. It scared the crap out of Pete. And it's totally not like the stuff that normally happens. "

Jinx looked at Jackson in surprise and saw that his eyebrows were raised too. "Wait. Your ghost is normally friends with everyone?" Jackson asked. A small smile dangled on his lips, and Jinx could tell he was trying to hide it.

"Yeah. He's always been a nice ghost. My dad says his name is John. Normally, he's just mischievous. Like, he'll move your car keys from one place to another, and my dad swears he can hear him giggling about it." He smiled shyly at Jackson and Jinx. "I know it sounds crazy . . . But anyway, we just don't understand why all of a sudden things have gotten bad."

Jinx said, trying hard not to sound too friendly, "Are you sure this Pete guy wasn't making this up? Was he super drunk?"

Todd's face turned somber. "No way. Pete barely ever drinks. He's good friends with my parents and comes in to talk my dad up while he's at the bar. He normally orders club soda. And anyway, he's not the only one who has noticed the change. My cousin Michael is our busboy. He quit because he won't go down to the basement anymore to get supplies. Every time he goes down there, something flies at him. He's had about six black eyes. He was never afraid of the ghost before, because there was nothing to be afraid of. Now it's just downright dangerous."

Jinx asked, "Are you sure it's not another ghost? A different entity, maybe?"

Todd shook his head. "No, the patrons and my parents say they can hear John's laugh. I haven't heard it yet, but they have. They say it's him, all right, but a really mean version of him. None of us understands what's going on."

Jinx thought hard for a second. *This could be an amazing case.* She twisted her lip and stayed quiet. Then she made a decision. A decision that had nothing to do with Todd's long eyelashes and tousled hair.

"We'll do it."

Jackson cleared his throat, annoyed.

"What?" she asked.

He shook his head. "Nothing. Just maybe you should ask the entire team before you make final decisions."

"OK, OK. Team—what do you think?"

Jackson turned toward Todd, grinning. "We'll do it."

CHAPTER 4

Jinx walked to her next class in a daze, working out the logistics of the next few days. After chatting with Todd some more, the three of them had decided that the upcoming Friday would be the night that Jackson and Jinx would spend at the bar. Jinx had to think of another "friend's" house to stay overnight at for her parents. Last time, they had been so happy to learn that Jinx *had* a friend besides Jackson, they didn't ask her any questions. They'd even dropped her off at the apartment building. This time would be trickier. She doubted even her laid-back dad would agree to her spending all night in a pub.

She headed into her English class and sat behind Haley, the school's most popular cheerleader—and Jinx's worst enemy. Haley used to invite Jackson to parties all the time in middle school, sometimes right in front of her. She'd never asked Jinx, even when Jinx was standing right there.

Jinx flopped into her seat, accidentally bumping into Haley's desk. Haley turned around and shot her a dirty look. Jinx stared back and knocked the desk forward again. Haley turned to the front with a huff, and Jinx smiled to herself. *Score one for the weird girl*, she thought.

Haley turned to the girl sitting across from her, another cheerleader. "Maddie, I think that new cheer we made for Todd is totally gonna help him."

Maddie nodded, and Jinx tried to tune them out. Everything about their voices made her cringe. She scowled to herself and started to make a list of things they'd need for the overnight. Jinx's stomach butterflied as she thought of spending the night at Todd's tavern. He had seemed nice, and he didn't once seem like he thought she was crazy or awful. Or worse, boring. He'd definitely been into the conversation. Jinx's mind drifted off into a daydream. One with ghosts and her ghost-hunting equipment and maybe, just maybe, Todd's lips . . .

Fingers snapped in front of her face. Startled, she sat up and dropped her pencil. She expected it to be her English teacher, Ms. Owen, who was tough about daydreaming in class. Instead, she looked into the big blue eyes of Haley.

"Hellooo?" Haley said. "That must have been some fantasy." She looked over at Maddie, and the two giggled.

"Never. Snap. Your. Fingers. At. Me. Again," Jinx said through clenched teeth.

Haley's eyes grew wide in mock alarm. "Whoa, you're *so* scary." She snickered at Maddie again. "I forgot your name, and I need to ask you a question. But you were way off in dreamland."

Jinx couldn't believe it. She'd forgotten her name? She'd even forgotten her *new* name? Leave it to Haley to be *that* oblivious to everyone but herself.

"Well, if the question is 'do I look fat in this outfit?' the answer is yes." Jinx knew exactly where to hit Haley. And if Haley didn't remember who she was, well . . . there was nothing she could fire back with.

Sure enough, Haley's face hardened. It was her turn to clench her teeth. She spit out at her, "Were you sitting with Jackson and Todd at a picnic table fourth period?"

Jinx leaned in. "What's it to you?"

"*Because*, I wanted to know if he is starting on Friday. But that was dumb of me. I don't know why he'd tell you anything. He probably hit his head during practice and thought you were his mom or something."

Haley glanced down at the paper Jinx was writing on. Jinx had written an equipment list with supplies like a toothbrush and sleeping bag. She had also written *Todd* in the upper right-hand corner, surrounded by a 3-D box. Jinx didn't even remember writing that.

"What. Is. This," Haley said. "Ohhh my god, what are you writing, you freak?"

Jinx smiled. "Oh, nothing. Just a list of things I need when I spend the night at Todd's parents' bar this Friday. After the game, of course." Jinx couldn't help it—she decided to dig in further. "Oh, and he *is* starting." She had no idea, but it was a fifty-fifty shot anyway.

Jinx knew Todd and Haley had dated a while ago. And while Jinx had told Jackson she couldn't care less about school gossip, the truth was, she loved it. So she also knew that Todd had broken up with Haley, but everyone thought Haley still had a thing for him.

Another reason to help Todd. The boy had good taste. Or could at least fix his mistakes.

Haley's eyes widened, and she flipped around in her seat. Even Haley's pet, Maddie, had nothing to say to that. Jinx gave herself a mental pat on the back. *Now let's see if you forget me*, she thought.

As Ms. Owen swept into the room, Jinx felt a wave of regret wash over her. Not because of Haley, but because of Todd. It wasn't very professional to break confidentiality. And although she'd never promised to keep the haunting a secret, it was bad form to use his situation to her advantage.

Her heart sank. Maybe Haley wouldn't forget who Jinx was again, but she might also be harming her chances for a heavier caseload. If people thought she was a blabbermouth, who would come to her for an investigation? And then, of course, there was the idea that she might have hurt Todd, a thought Jinx tried hard not to dwell on.

Ms. Owen began speaking in front of her class. "All right, today we start a new unit. Plays. Anyone heard of *Death of a Salesman*?"

Jinx wondered if the play had the death of a love life in it, too.

Chapter 5

The pass went wide yet again. Jackson did everything he could to catch it, even though it was just a drill. He just didn't want Todd to get yelled at again. The quarterback was definitely off his game.

The whole team was mad at Todd. They had a big game on Friday, and no one knew whether or not Coach would start Todd. He was their best player, but he couldn't seem to get it together.

After practice, Todd didn't look up at

anyone as they walked to the locker room. The team was unusually quiet. Normally it was like a small army walking in. Now, it moved inside like a funeral procession. As the players passed the office, Coach motioned to Todd. Todd hung his head and went into the office like a man on death row. Jackson pretended to get a drink of water near the office to try to hear what Coach was saying. Things like:

"Todd, what the heck is going on out there?"

Jackson didn't hear a reply. Two of his teammates walked by, so he pretended to tie a shoe by the door.

The coach went on, "My ninety-year-old grandma plays better football than you did today. Every pass went wide, and you missed six snaps. Where's your head? We play East tomorrow, and we need you on board."

Todd still didn't say anything. Jackson gave up all pretense and stood near the door, his ear pressed against the wood.

The coach's voice took on a different tone. A concerned tone. "Listen, Todd, the recruiter from State will be here next Friday. If you want to get that scholarship, you have to ramp up your performance. After this past coupla weeks, I gotta say, son, I'm worried. Is everything OK?"

The office grew quiet. Then Jackson heard Todd say, "Things are a little messed up for me right now. But I think I've figured out how to make it better."

Jackson heard the coach sigh. "Well, I'll start you tomorrow, Todd, but if it's like practice today, I'm putting Jackson in. Got it? And if it stays like this, Jackson starts next Friday, too. Even if he is a sophomore. We need some consistency. Get your head on straight and come ready to play tomorrow. Show us what you've got."

The door handle turned, and Jackson jumped away. He hadn't expected the conversation to end so soon.

He ducked around the corner just in time to watch Todd come out of the office. Jackson felt like a sneak. He was truly concerned about Todd, though—even though Jackson would have loved to start, he knew the team needed its regular QB. And more than ever, Todd needed the team.

As Todd passed Jackson, he didn't even turn his head. Still, Jackson could see that his eyes were wet and red.

Todd went to his locker and started taking off his pads. One by one, members of the team left the row of lockers, stealing glances at Todd but not saying anything. Soon it was just Jackson and Todd left.

Showered and dressed, Jackson went up to Todd.

"Listen, I heard what Coach said. And we need you, dude. Jinx and I are going to make this right, I promise." Jackson set his jaw. He meant every word.

Todd looked up at him, tears threatening at the corners of his eyes. "That's good, man. Because I don't think I can take much more of this." He cleared his throat. "I need that scholarship! If I don't get it because of some stupid ghost . . . well, maybe I don't deserve it then."

Jackson slapped him on the shoulder. "That's not going to happen. You deserve that scholarship just like your parents deserve a bar that is still running. I promise you, we will make this better."

Todd looked at Jackson in relief. "No pressure, man, but I'm counting on you. If you don't get rid of this ghost, my life will be ruined."

Jackson looked away. *No pressure.*

CHAPTER 6

"Sleeping bag?"
     Jinx read from the list like a drill sergeant.

"Check." Jackson patted his bag.

"Toothbrush and toothpaste?"

"Check and check."

"Banishing stones?"

"Check." Jackson had no idea if the stones worked—he'd just ordered them from the back of a catalog—but he did have them.

"Night goggles?"

Jackson almost said check, but then looked down at his duffel bag. No telltale goggle bulge. He thought about where he'd put them, but couldn't remember—he could have sworn he'd put them in the bag.

He had found the goggles in the attic just a few months ago and knew immediately that they would be perfect on the next case. They had been his dad's during his military time, so Jackson had a lot of sentimental feelings for them. But he couldn't find them. He started rifling through his bag one more time, frantic, resolving to try his closet if he couldn't find them. He would tear apart the attic again if he had to.

Just then, the light switched off and something grabbed his shoulder.

"Boo!" yelled Jinx. Jackson knew what that meant. He sighed.

"Very funny, Jinx. Don't play with those, you'll break them." After his talk with Todd, Jackson wasn't in the mood.

Jinx snorted, then turned on the lights. She dangled the goggles by the strap from a finger of her left hand. "They seem pretty much indestructible. Why are you so cranky, anyway?" She threw the goggles to Jackson, who caught them and swooped them into his bag before Jinx got an idea to play hide-and-seek. He shrugged off her question.

"Those are cool, Jackson. I'm so glad you found them. Especially if we're in for a wild night."

Jackson's arms broke out into goose bumps. Todd's description of the ghost's recent activity had been spooky. He was glad they had the goggles too. He was almost sad to leave the comfort of his own room—something he'd never in a million years admit to Jinx—but the idea that ghosts were making contact with people—even if they were throwing glasses— gave Jackson hope. If he could figure it out, maybe someday he could contact his dad.

"OK!" Jinx clapped her hands together. "I think we're good to go. Black Eagle Tavern, here we come!"

Jinx began loading everything on her back. Jackson thought she seemed extra eager to

start the case. He had a sneaking suspicion
it had to do with Todd, and a strange feeling
pinched him. He pushed it away. She was
probably just excited because she'd have lots to
blog about. Although her hair did seem extra
combed. He stared at her sideways.

She was all loaded up and eating a Twizzler
loudly. She looked at Jackson and, with her
mouth full and bright red, said, "Wha?"

Jackson just smiled. "Let's go. We're going
to be late."

Jinx rolled her eyes. "Yeah, and we wouldn't
want to offend the ghost."

It was a short trip to the bar, but Jinx shrunk
down in Jackson's car anyway, on the off
chance she would see her parents out driving
around. Even though it was two in the
morning. She had told them she was going
to Haley's house to spend the night and that
Jackson, Haley, and she were going to a movie
first, so Jackson would drop her off. Jackson
thought the ducking down was a little overkill,
but he knew her parents would be super mad

if they knew what she was doing. And since it *was* two in the morning, it would look extra suspicious. Jackson was glad his mom wasn't quite so tough to get around.

When they got to the bar, Todd greeted them at the door and let them in. All the lights were on. Jackson took in the decor. Wood paneling everywhere, except behind the bar itself, which had a huge mirror that looked way too fancy for the rest of the place, and shelves with tons of liquor and glasses. The carpet was red and at one time probably really bright, but the color had faded to a muddy brown in many spots. Wooden booths snuggled against the walls, and vintage advertising signs hung between windows.

Nothing fancy or pretentious about this place, Jackson thought. He immediately liked it.

Jinx was frowning, though. Jackson nudged her. "What?"

She shook her head. "I don't know . . ."

Todd had been putting their stuff in the corner and came back around. He looked at Jinx, and she smiled.

Jackson did a double-take. She smiled! And it didn't even seem sarcastic! What was going on?

Todd asked, "Is there something wrong?"

In a move Jackson hadn't seen since middle school, Jinx smoothed her hair behind her ears. She shook her head. "It's just . . . I don't feel anything, you know?"

Todd's eyebrows furrowed. "Yeah, actually, I do. It feels different in here tonight. And nothing weird happened. I don't get it."

Jackson poked his head through the strangely small gap between Todd and Jinx. "Maybe he knew we were coming?"

Todd laughed. "Yeah. Maybe."

Jinx, though, had become all business. "OK, I'm setting up the video cameras here and here." She pointed at the front of the bar and the open door to the basement. "If I had the infrared camera . . ." She sighed. "Anyway, Jackson and I will sweep the area with the EMF and EVP about every hour. We'll also talk and see if we can't get a reaction from the ghost."

She bit her lip and paused. "You don't have to stay here, actually, if you don't want to." Jackson thought her expression looked a little too hopeful.

"Are you sure?" Todd said. "I don't want to bail on you or anything. But, truthfully, I could use some sleep. My brother's out of town, and we've been sharing a room—I think I could actually sleep the whole night without him coming in at odd hours."

Jackson looked at his watch. "It's two a.m. He comes home later than this?"

Todd nodded glumly. "He . . . well, he has stuff he needs to do, I guess."

Jinx stared at Todd with sympathy. "Well, I don't think you're pulling a hoax, so go home and sleep. We'll report to you in the morning."

Todd's relief was palpable. He gathered up his stuff. "OK, sounds good. I hope something happens . . . but not something bad. Thanks again for doing this for me."

Jinx gave him a big smile. "No problem!" Then she seemed to catch herself and said, "And anyway, you'll be returning the favor on our website." She cleared her throat and looked down at her EVP monitor for the thousandth time.

Todd nodded and waved. "See you tomorrow."

Jackson thought Jinx stared at his back awfully hard as he left.

CHAPTER 7

Jinx woke up with a start. Drool ran down her chin, and she wiped it off and snuggled deeper in her sleeping bag. The smell of stale beer wafted all around her. She wrinkled her nose in disgust. *Sleeping on a bar floor? Even worse than camping, she decided.*

A gray light lit up the room, and for a moment Jinx thought it looked otherworldly. She grabbed the EMF monitor and pointed it around. Then she realized it was just the usual glow that appeared before dawn. She set down the EMF monitor in disappointment and checked the clock on her phone. Six-thirty. And not a single thing had happened in the bar. Nothing even slightly paranormal. Not even a mischievous laugh.

She glanced over at Jackson, who was sleeping on his back, his mouth hanging open. She laughed a little to herself—he'd slept that way since he was six. Then she rolled onto her own back and thought about the night.

About how nothing had happened.

Was Todd lying? Jinx tried to figure out why he would, but she couldn't come up with anything. From what he'd said, other people had even seen and heard things. Could it be a case of mass craziness? Maybe they had all just talked themselves into it. Or maybe Todd just made the whole thing up. Or maybe Todd's parents were spooking people to get the bar some more attention. Though that didn't make much sense, since they were losing patrons . . . Jinx just couldn't think of a reason anyone would make up this kind of haunting.

She got up and squatted down beside Jackson. She said in her loudest voice, "*Jackson.*"

He sat up so fast she fell over on her butt. But she would have fallen anyway, she was laughing so hard. Jackson looked around, wild-eyed and bewildered. His hair stuck straight up in the front and was smooshed flat in the back.

After Jackson seemed to get his bearings, he flipped the sleeping bag off of his legs and stood up.

"Oh, real funny, Jinx. You could have given me a heart attack."

Jinx stood up too. Wiping her eyes, she said, "Yeah, well then at least something would have happened tonight."

Jackson yawned and stretched. "Nothing on the equipment?"

Jinx was already packing up the cameras. "I'll check tonight, but I'm pretty sure there was not a thing."

Jackson yawned again and shook his head. He started rolling up his sleeping bag.

"So, can you think of any reason Todd would lie to us about this stuff?" Jinx said carefully. After their fight about Jinx not trusting anyone, even Jackson, she knew he was sensitive to any sign that she was up to her old habits. But a puzzled look crossed Jackson's face. He shook his head. "I can't think of any reason why he would."

He actually thought about it, instead of trusting blindly, Jinx thought. *Maybe by our one hundredth case, the two of us will combine to make a normal person.*

Jinx twisted her lip. "Yeah, I can't think of any reason either. But I think it's time for some reconnaissance."

Jackson folded up the cameras and stuffed them in their bags. "What do you mean?"

"I mean," said Jinx, "we need to get the names and locations of the bar patrons who have heard things and ask them about it. See if this is something that people are talking themselves into."

Jackson nodded slowly. "Yeah, that might be a good idea. What about the glasses shattering and Michael's black eyes, though? That can't be people making it up."

Jinx shook her head. "I'm not sure. I just know that something is up here, and we need to find out what it is."

Jackson gathered up his gear and put it on his back. Walking out, he started ruffling Jinx's hair. She ducked, almost hitting the doorframe, and swatted his hand away.

Jackson chuckled. "Well, whatever's up, Veronica Mars, we'll get to the bottom of it. But first, let's get breakfast. Not being scared out of my dome makes me hungry, I guess."

Jinx smiled. Breathing made Jackson hungry, but breakfast was a good idea anyway.

CHAPTER 8

Pete, the club-soda drinker, was pretty burly, it turned out. So was his wife, Beth. But both were the nicest people Jinx had ever met. She sat on the sofa and sipped her tea awkwardly. She hated going into strange people's houses and making small talk. She could feel Jackson grinning at her discomfort. It was totally unfair—getting along with people was so easy for Jackson. She purposefully spilled a little tea on his pant leg.

"So, what brings you here again?" Beth asked. "Not that we mind. We never had any children ourselves, so we love getting visits from young people." She smiled, and her whole face lit up. Jinx couldn't help but smile back.

She cleared her throat and said, "Well, we heard that a while back at the Black Eagle, when Pete was taking a—"

Jackson cut her off and said, "We heard that some strange things have happened to you at the Black Eagle Tavern. Is that true?"

"You bet it's true," Pete said. "Even my Bethy here had a little experience. We never told anyone, but she came in to see me at the bar. While she was waiting, this glass moved right on its own and smashed into the floor."

Beth chimed in. "Scared me to death! I almost hightailed it outta there, but I couldn't leave my Pete. Besides, I thought it was just John playing tricks. Only, he never actually smashed a glass before. That worried me, truth be told." She put her hand on Pete's arm and patted it. He covered her hand with his and squeezed.

Any more of this and I'm going to get a cavity, Jinx thought. As if reading her mind, Jackson nudged her again.

"You don't think that . . . well, you don't think that something else could explain these things besides a ghost . . . I mean, um, John?" Jinx asked.

Pete said, "Nope. The Black Eagle has always been haunted. But John has always been friendly. It's always felt downright homey in there, and John was a part of that. But this new feeling in there is . . . well, it's a dangerous feeling. Something mean. I've never felt that before in there."

Beth looked angry for a second. "I mean, really. Whoever would try to hurt me and Pete? We never hurt anyone! We don't deserve that sort of thing. Though God knows most people don't."

Jinx agreed, about Pete and Beth at least. Despite herself, she was really starting to like these people.

"When did it start feeling dangerous in there?" Jackson asked.

Beth and Pete looked at each other again. Beth sniffed. "Well, listen. I'm a good, churchgoing woman, and I don't like to gossip."

There was a heavy pause in the room as she refrained from gossiping. Jinx counted to three in her head, and sure enough, Beth continued. In Jinx's experience, people who said they didn't like to gossip were always the best gossipers around.

"But if you ask me," Beth said, "it's when that brother of his came back to town. Now mind, it didn't happen right away. But right after Todd and Devon started fighting—"

Jinx interrupted, "Todd and Devon fight a lot?"

Pete laughed hard. "Like two roosters in a barnyard." Having never been to a farm, Jinx guessed that meant fairly often.

"But only since Devon moved back," Beth continued. "Those two used to be inseparable. Now they can't seem to stay in the same room together for more than ten minutes."

Jinx took a sip of her now-cold tea. "What do they fight about?"

Beth glanced downward. "That's a private matter, surely," she said.

Jackson leaned forward and said, softly, "But if they're fighting in public, it can't be *that* private, can it?"

Jinx could have kissed him. She'd had no idea how to counter what Beth said. But Jackson could be a genius with that sort of thing. Somehow, Jinx's mind wandered off into thinking about Todd. Imaginary Todd, leaning down to kiss her after she'd saved him from some flying glassware—and then Jackson's face popped up in place of Todd's. She snapped out of it. What was happening to her?

"—with needles everywhere." Beth finished up.

Jinx had missed the whole explanation. Jackson looked at her curiously. "So this is pretty new, huh?" he asked Beth.

Pete nodded. "Oh yeah. Devon was the varsity quarterback, just like Todd. And he got a scholarship to Portland State. He blew his knee, though, last semester. Lost his scholarship. He came home to make some money. But he can't keep it. Not with the problem he has."

Jinx was a little lost. What problem had she missed?

Jackson sighed. "It's just sad to see something like that. Well, I think we should get going. We want to talk to the busboy, Michael, too."

Beth's eyes sparkled. "Tell him hi from me!"

Pete guffawed. "The missus here thinks he's mighty fine-looking. Mangy little kid, if you ask me."

Both Beth and Pete chuckled together, and soon they had Jackson and Jinx laughing too. They walked to the door, and Beth enveloped them both in hugs. "Don't be strangers, now!"

They walked out the door and into the light.

"A *drug* problem?" Jinx said again.

"For the millionth time, yes," Jackson sighed. "You really need to listen to people when they talk."

"What?" Jinx replied. "OK, so let me get this straight. Devon is a big deal in high school, goes to Portland State on a scholarship, blows out his knee, and then gets addicted to painkillers?"

Jackson nodded. "It's so sad. I'd forgotten, but I'd read about Devon in the paper. PSU was thinking of starting him as a freshman."

He looked at Jinx expectantly. She said, "And that's a big deal?"

"Yes that's a big deal!"

"OK, OK. I'm not a meathead like you."

Jackson smiled. Jinx went on, "So, this starts when Devon comes back, but only after Devon and Todd start fighting. Maybe it's not a ghost at all. Maybe it's a poltergeist instead."

Jackson looked puzzled. "Explain the difference to me again?"

Jinx put on her best teacher voice. "OK, a poltergeist is just bad energy that gets manifested from someone going through a rocky emotional time. Like, for instance, two brothers, who have been close, fighting because one of them has a drug problem." She looked at Jackson, eyebrows raised, and then went on. "But a haunting is by a spirit that hasn't moved on to the light. This Black Eagle situation totally sounds like a poltergeist."

Jackson looked out at the sky, thinking about the new theory. Then he added, "But people say the bar has been haunted for years. And what about your research?"

"Well, all I'd heard about this haunting before this is that people got a 'good feeling.' There's no supernatural force behind positive vibes—I feel good when I go to Voodoo Donut, but that doesn't mean I think it's haunted." She paused for a second and twisted her lip. "Although, supposedly, these things happen during puberty, not this late."

Jackson frowned. "Yeah, a lot of this isn't adding up. Let's talk to Michael. Maybe he can shed some light on things."

Jinx smiled. "Well, we wouldn't want to disappoint Beth. We did say we'd say hi to him."

Jackson grinned back.

CHAPTER 9

Even Jackson admitted to himself that Michael was good-looking. But good-looking or not, Michael looked like every other biking Portlandian—beard, flannel shirt, and one pant leg folded up.

"Beth says hi," Jackson said after they had introduced themselves. They'd met Michael at a bike-repair place slash coffee shop. He sat outside on the patio, tinkering with his fixed gear.

Jinx moved the straw around in her

ridiculously huge coffee drink, pushing it through the mountain of whipped cream on top. She tried to catch the straw with her mouth, but it traveled away along the edge of the cup. Jackson had a hard time not laughing.

Michael rolled his eyes. "Yeah, Beth has a fake crush on me, I guess. But she's cool."

Jackson took a drink of his coffee. Decaffeinated, so he wouldn't be bouncing off the walls afterward. He tried not to get annoyed that Michael hadn't stopped swapping out bike parts.

"So, you stopped working at the Black Eagle because of things . . . happening?" Jackson asked.

Michael put his wrench down and stared at Jinx and Jackson. "You bet I did. I swear, I almost got killed in that basement one night."

Jinx leaned forward with a smear of whipped cream on her upper lip. "So what exactly happened, then?"

Michael sat up in his chair. "There were a lot of things that happened, at least lately. But the clincher for me was about a week ago."

Jackson leaned forward too.

Michael went on, "I felt bad about quitting because my uncle was doing me a favor, but this was too much." He tapped his fingers on the table. "I went downstairs like usual to get some beer. We always run out on Fridays because that's when some of the college kids come in. Anyway, I'm in the basement, looking for the beer, when the cooler door shuts."

"You were stuck in the cooler?" Jackson asked.

Michael nodded, and Jinx let out a huff of air, scattering specs of whipped cream on the sidewalk. "And I bet there's no handle on the inside," she said.

Michael nodded again, solemnly. "Yeah, I was stuck. And freaked out because I was already freezing and I had short sleeves on. Then stuff started flying. I got another black eye when a bag of fries smashed right into my face."

"Just like that? Things started to fly?" Jackson asked. Jinx slurped up a huge gulp of iced mocha.

Michael nodded. "Yeah, it was the worst it had ever been. And I kept yelling, trying to get someone to let me out, but Devon and Todd were yelling so loud at each other upstairs that it took them a while to hear me. I was totally trapped."

Jackson shivered.

"After about ten minutes, a case of beer came flying off the shelf and hit me in the head," Michael continued. "It knocked me out. The next thing I knew, some paramedics were standing over me, holding ice bags. I was covered with a blanket. It was scary, man."

Jinx seemed lost in thought. "Devon and Todd were fighting? You could hear them upstairs?"

Michael nodded. "You could've heard them on Mars. When don't they fight lately?"

Jinx looked at Jackson and mouthed, "poltergeist." But Jackson still wasn't convinced. "When other bad things have happened to you, were Todd and Devon around?"

"Now that I think about it, yes," Michael said.

Jinx looked at Jackson knowingly. "And before Devon came back, were there other weird incidents?"

Michael nodded. Jinx looked surprised, and Jackson smiled to himself. Jinx wasn't used to not being right.

"What things?" she demanded.

"Well, just things being moved around," Michael said. "Like, mischievous, but not mean, you know? It always felt like something nice. *He* always seemed nice. His name is John." His face turned red. "I probably sound crazy, but I'm not. I grew up in that bar— John's always been there. But he always felt like . . . a mascot or something. Never mean. Even protective, if that makes any sense."

Jackson looked at Jinx. He knew without saying anything that they were thinking the same thing. This many people believed in one ghost? Maybe it was mass hysteria. Even Jackson was skeptical about the existence of ghosts sometimes. He'd never encountered an entire group of people who just accepted a ghost in their presence. Even a nice one.

Still, the fact that so many people had seen things happen meant there was a good chance that something supernatural actually was happening.

Jackson stood up. "Well, we won't take up more of your time." Jinx grabbed her huge drink and stood by Jackson. "Thanks for talking to us."

Michael stood up, too, and shook both their hands. "Yeah, man, no problem. I hope you fix whatever's going on. People are starting to abandon the bar, and that's really bad for my aunt and uncle. And for Todd."

Jackson nodded. "We hope so, too."

CHAPTER 10

"You want me to what?" Todd ran his hand through his hair. Jackson shifted on his feet.

"I know it sounds crazy, but nothing happened the night we stayed there. Nothing. Not even a temperature shift. And after talking to others who have had weird experiences . . . it seems that whatever is happening is happening because of you and your brother."

The picnic table shifted as Jinx plunked down cross-legged on the bench. She had on her "deal with it" look, but her hands fiddled with her hair more often than Jackson had ever seen.

After their talk with Michael, the two had decided to spend another night in the pub. This time, though, they'd have Todd and Devon stay the night, too. And since it seemed that the brothers couldn't be in the same room and not fight, Jinx and Jackson thought there was a good possibility they might actually get some ghostly action. Plus, Jackson noticed, the idea of Todd spending the night in the same room with her didn't seem to bother Jinx one bit. The pang he had felt before hit him again, but he pushed it down again. It was time for work.

Todd was shaking his head, his knee bouncing up and down. "I don't know if I can get my brother to come. He's not the most reliable right now."

Jackson cleared his throat and made the decision to tell Todd what they knew. "Look, man, we know why he's been so . . . hard to deal with lately."

Todd looked down at the table. "I'm not surprised. Portland can be a small town sometimes, when you know people."

"Or when you're featured in the paper," Jinx chimed in. In an uncharacteristically soft voice, she added, "It must be hard for you."

Since when had she been sensitive? Jackson wondered. The Jinx he knew wasn't exactly good at empathy. He stared at her until she looked at him and mouthed, "what?" Jackson looked back to Todd. The quarterback's eyes were shiny, bright, and wounded.

"You have no idea," Todd said. "Dev and I used to be so close. I don't even know who he is any more. He won't listen to me. He keeps stealing money... I don't know what to do." Jackson had never seen a more miserable expression in his life. He patted Todd on the back.

"Well, first, we'll talk to this ghost."

"Poltergeist," Jinx chirped.

Jackson looked pointedly at Jinx. The last thing Todd needed was someone telling him *he* was doing all these bad things and driving his parents' business away. Even if it was true. And anyway, Jackson just wasn't sold on the poltergeist thing.

"So here's the deal," Jackson said. "We'll plan for this Thursday night. You try to talk your brother into coming. Just text us around bar close, let us know if he won't come, and we'll try for another time."

Todd nodded. "I'll do my best, but I'm not promising anything. Thursdays are typically when he scores." Todd let out a sharp, bitter laugh. "That used to mean something about football, but now. . . ." He got up and threw his backpack over his shoulder. "Thursday, then. Maybe this will actually be resolved in time for the big game." He walked away, shoulders slumped.

"Big game?" Jinx asked.

Jackson said, "A college recruiter's coming by for Friday's game. That's why I thought we could do Thursday. Maybe have a chance to put an end to things for Todd before he loses his shot at college ball."

Jinx sighed. "That makes sense, though

Thursday is next to impossible for me. Guess it's another lie for my parents, then." She opened a bag of Twizzlers and snapped off a piece with her teeth. "I wonder what I should wear?"

Jackson stared at her, disbelieving. "Are *you* on drugs?"

"I just mean—" Jinx stammered, "what I should wear in case I get stuck in a cooler. Duh." She dropped her Twizzler and, in the process of getting another one, knocked her own bag off the table.

Jackson shook his head. "Who needs a ghost when we have our very own Jinx to throw things around?"

She smacked him in the head with a new Twizzler.

CHAPTER 11

With the equipment set up and the lights dimmed in the bar, all Jinx and Jackson could do was wait. Todd paced through the bar, back and forth, back and forth, waiting for his brother to come in. It was already two-thirty, and Devon hadn't showed. Jinx had given up hope, but Todd wouldn't let them leave. He kept muttering mysteriously, "He'll come. I made it impossible for him not to."

Jinx didn't mind that much, anyway. What else was she going to do? She used the time to tinker on her computer. She was in the middle of making T-shirts with the Paranormalists logo and motto on them. After that, she'd have to add a merch page and some buy buttons to the website. She could hardly wait. Jackson thought she was being premature, but she thought being prepared was better than not having shirts handy. Plus, she'd gotten more than a hundred hits on her last post! And if anything actually happened on this case, she thought that Todd's brown eyes—and his story, of course—would help boost their popularity. Maybe she'd post footage from the camera on YouTube, too, and see if she could get followers that way...

Just as she was about to drag the logo onto the T-shirts on the CafePress site, her computer flickered.

She looked over to Todd and Jackson. Both boys stared at their phones, which were flickering on and off.

Just then the door slammed open, making Jinx jump so high she almost crashed her laptop on the floor. She put her hand over her heart and tried to slow her breathing.

It was Devon. Looking a little worse for wear.

The lights in the bar blinked. Jinx looked at Jackson and tried to telepathically tell him she told him so. *This definitely has to be a poltergeist*, she thought. Devon's crazy energy had to be causing the disturbances.

Just as she had the thought, Jackson pointed to her EMF device sitting near her foot. "Jinx . . ." he said. Jinx looked down. The EMF meter was glowing bright red, the needle almost snapping off, it was so far over. Jinx sat straight up and felt the hair on her head stand on end.

The temperature dropped, and she saw Jackson shiver.

But Todd and Devon seemed completely unaware of the change in the atmosphere. Devon looked at Todd with narrowed, bloodshot eyes and said, "Where is he? Where's this guy who had stuff for me?"

Todd's face was still, and he didn't say a word.

Devon shook his head, and an expression of disgust took over his face. "You lied to me, didn't you?" He looked around the room. "And for what? What weird game do you and your little friends think you're playing?"

Todd stepped forward. "That's hysterical, you being mad at *me* for lying. That's all you've done for the past few weeks!"

The temperature dropped even further. Without thinking, Jinx and Jackson moved closer together. "Your cameras are going, yeah?" he whispered. She nodded, knowing she must have looked pale. The EMF meter vibrated so hard that Jinx had a hard time keeping hold of it. Jackson picked up the EVP recorder. Jinx could see the interior whirring like crazy. She knew when she looked at it back home it would be completely full of otherworldly voices.

"OK, I definitely don't think this is a poltergeist," Jinx whispered to Jackson. "None of this would register on the meters, especially the temperature drop."

Todd and Devon continued to argue, and

Jackson looked at them thoughtfully. "Yeah, but this definitely has something to do with what's going on between them."

A row of glasses on the bar started to shake.

"Uh, Todd?" Jackson said.

But Todd and Devon were too busy going at it to hear. "You're wasting your life! And you're taking me down with you, you know!" Todd was yelling. "You've lied, you've taken my money... But worse, you're killing yourself and you don't care at all!"

The bar started shaking harder, making everything clang together. "Hey guys!" Jackson said again. But Devon was yelling back.

"I don't need you judging me, too. You have no idea what I've been going through! You're supposed to be my brother and have my back. Instead, you're just like everyone else!"

"Well maybe everyone else is right!" Todd fired back. "What you've been 'going through' is making some stupid choices! You're embarrassing the whole family!"

The racket at the bar became deafening. Jinx knew the glass wouldn't last much longer. She put two fingers in her mouth and whistled high and long. It reverberated around the room, so loud it even drowned out the shaking of the glasses. She'd learned the trick when she was ten, and it had never been handier. Todd and Devon turned to her with wide eyes.

She looked at the bar, then back at Devon and Todd. "You may want to duck, is all I'm saying."

As the words left her mouth, three glasses came shooting from the bar, straight toward Devon and Todd. The brothers ducked, and the glasses shattered against a door behind them. Jinx felt someone flop on her as she threw her arms over her head. Two more glasses shattered against the door. Around the body on top of her, Jinx could see Devon and Todd army-crawling to one of the booths. One by one, each glass launched off the bar. Glass pieces littered the floor in front of the doorway, making it impossible to walk out. Until they picked up the debris, they were stuck.

Once things finally quieted, Jinx pinched the arm that draped over her. Jackson yelled "ouch!" and got off of her. She glared at him.

"Really, Knight in Shining Armor? I can't take care of myself? You don't get hurt by glass?"

Jackson shrugged. "It was instinct."

Jinx snorted and then watched Devon and Todd climb out from under the booth, both of them breathless.

"Well, you got your paranormal activity, anyway," Todd said.

Jinx laughed. "Yeah, I'll say." She added cheerfully, "This is going to be awesome on the website!"

Jackson shook his head, turning to Todd and Devon. "Whatever this is, it seems to revolve around you guys fighting."

The two brothers squinted at each other, a wary look on each of their faces. Jinx was struck by how much they resembled each other, even though Devon's frame was stick-thin, and dark circles hung under his eyes.

Suddenly, a hiss carried through the bar.

"Lissssteenn . . ." the voice said, the *s*'s carrying through the bar like a demonic snake.

Jackson crunched some of the glass piled around the door with a heel. "Something tells me this is going to be a long night."

CHAPTER 12

The word *listen* slithered through the bar again, and the four of them huddled together.

Jinx asked Todd, "Has your ghost ever spoken before? What are we supposed to listen to?"

Todd shook his head. "No, never. And I have no idea what that means." Then he looked over at his brother.

Devon's eyebrows furrowed. "Oh yeah, look at me, because it's probably all my fault."

Before Todd could respond, Jinx put her hands on the two brothers' chests. "Don't start again. Last time we got ambushed, remember?"

Both brothers slumped away and pouted.

"Let's figure this out," Jackson said. "Something has got to be triggering this ghost."

Jinx rolled her eyes. "Now you want to be the ghost's therapist?"

Jackson frowned at her. "Maybe this ghost had a brother or something. I don't know. Can't you look up your research about this bar?"

Jinx had to admit it was a good idea. And the brothers had stopped fighting for the time being. Even her precious equipment was quiet. It was as good a time as any.

She powered up her laptop and opened up the file about the Black Eagle Tavern. She'd gathered a few articles about the place but hadn't had a chance to read all of them. But just as she clicked open the folder, the lights went out completely.

The only thing lit in the room was her EMF equipment.

"It doesn't seem to want a background check," Todd said.

Jinx felt something swoosh by her ear, then heard the smash against the door. The smell of hard liquor filled the air. Jinx ducked down.

"Jackson," she hissed, "Now would be a good time for those night goggles, don't you think?"

Jackson's disembodied voice traveled to her. "Yep." She heard the sound of a zipper and then a snap and a whir.

"OK, got 'em on. Todd and Devon, move left. Put your hands out and you'll find the booth you were just under."

Another bottle whistled past Jinx's ear. The smash and sharp smell of alcohol filled the air again.

"Jinx, that was close," Jackson said, his voice shaky "You're right in the path where this thing is throwing things."

The word *listen* traveled around the room again.

Jackson continued guiding the group. "Crawl on your hands and knees to your right. You'll run right into the wall, and you can sit there."

Shaking, Jinx did what Jackson said and, sure enough, bumped into something solid. She wrapped her hands around her knees. Another bottle smashed against the wall.

"Jackson," Jinx whispered, "how are we going to get out of here?"

She felt someone grab her hand and knew it was him. She squeezed tightly, and he squeezed back. Another bottle smashed against the wall.

"Anybody's phone working?" Jackson asked.

Todd, Devon, and Jinx all said no. "Yeah, me neither," Jackson said with disappointment.

Then, from the booth, a small voice said, "Todd—you're right. I've made some bad choices. It's . . . just been really hard."

Quiet hung over the room for a moment, and then another bottle smashed. Jinx felt a shard of glass cut her cheek. *This assignment is turning out to be less fun than I thought*, she thought to herself. She crossed her fingers for some great footage. If they got out of there alive, she'd definitely upload it.

After a second, Todd whispered back to his brother. "I know it's been tough. And I haven't made it any easier for you."

"No, I know you're trying to help," Devon said quietly. "I should have listened to you before. But now . . . I don't know if I can stop. If I was stronger, maybe, but I'm not."

Jinx heard a bump, and Devon cried, "Ouch!"

Two more bottles smashed against the wall.

Todd's voice rose. "How could you say that, Devon?"

Jinx thought she could hear tears in Devon's voice. "What good am I?" he said. "I lost the scholarship. I can't help out the family. All I am is a burden! I'm useless! I can't even handle the pain without these painkillers . . ."

"Dev, you're the strongest person I know. *Of course* you can beat this thing. So you blew out your knee—so what? That wasn't your fault!"

Devon, sounding like he was fully crying, said, "But you're my little brother, Todd. I'm supposed to protect you. I should be better than I am. I should be someone you can turn to."

Todd sighed. "We're brothers. We help each other. You have a problem, a disease. You just need *help*. It's unfair of me to blame you for things. It's just . . ."—silence hung in the air for a minute—"I didn't know what to do, Dev. I could see you falling, and you wouldn't let me catch you." He choked up, and Jinx could feel a lump forming in her throat, too. As if he knew, Jackson squeezed Jinx's hand.

"It's my turn to help you this time," Todd continued. "We'll get you into a program. You can turn this thing around, I know it."

After a moment of quiet, Devon said, "OK, Todd. I can do it—if you help me. I'll get help. Tomorrow, even, I'll go."

Suddenly, the bottles stopped smashing.

Jinx could hear the drip, drip of liquor flowing off the bar and down the door. For a minute, nothing happened. And all of a sudden, the lights snapped back on.

CHAPTER 13

Jackson yelled, "Yeow!" and ripped the night goggles off his face. He rubbed his eyes with both hands, letting go of Jinx's hand. "Would have been nice to have a little warning about putting the lights back on," he mumbled.

He could hear Jinx giggling, and he shoved into her with his shoulder.

Through stinging eyes, he saw Todd and Devon getting up from underneath the booth. Both boys' eyes were red-rimmed. But Jackson thought they also both looked like a huge weight had been lifted from their shoulders.

"Is it over?" Devon asked.

Jinx was already up and checking her equipment. Though the EMF meter still showed some activity, the meter was not in the red. "I think we're OK now," she said. Jackson nodded. He didn't know why, but he was pretty sure that whatever was haunting the place was done smashing things. The place felt downright homey, just the way the bar patrons had described it.

He looked over to the door, where a huge pile of glass blocked the door. Drips of alcohol of all colors traveled down the wood paneling. The sharp smells filled his nose with every breath.

Todd grinned at Devon and said, "This is going to be a hard one to explain to Mom and Dad."

Devon laughed. "I'll buy us some more liquor and glasses before they get here. And we'll clean this up. Though the smell might stay around . . ."

Todd's face turned serious. "Honestly, I don't think they'll care. As long as they know we're all right. Both of us."

Devon swallowed and nodded. "Yeah. We're pretty lucky to have people who care about us." The brothers looked at each other, and Todd slapped Devon's shoulder.

Jackson watched Jinx go to her laptop to make sure it wasn't damaged. He honestly didn't know how she'd live without her computer. Within seconds, Jinx was engrossed in whatever was on the screen.

Jackson, Devon, and Todd started cleaning up. The sound of clinking glass filled the room. Soon Jackson was joking with the brothers about accidentally getting drunk from all the alcohol fumes. He made sure to walk carefully around the huge pile, hoping he wasn't just grinding glass into the floor.

"Hey, Jinx," he called over, "maybe you want to get off your butt and help us clean?"

Jinx held up one palm. "I'm researching." Devon and Todd shared a small smirk.

"Hey guys," Jinx said suddenly, sitting

up in her chair. "Listen to this." The others paused as Jinx continued. "So, according to this article from 1984, the person who owned this bar before died here."

Todd and Devon looked to each other. "Well, duh. That was John," Todd said. "Right, Dev?"

Devon nodded. "Oh, yeah. That's where Mom and Dad got the name from. I could never really tell if they actually thought it was the guy's spirit, but they always joked that it was cool to have a ghost around."

Todd smiled. "Yeah, although I don't think they had nights like tonight in mind."

"Wait," Jinx said, "it gets better. Er, sort of. Guess what the guy died from?"

Jackson, Devon, and Todd all looked at her expectantly.

"A drug overdose."

No one moved for a minute. Jinx went on. According the article, John was survived by a brother.

"All he says in the article is that he could never convince John to get help," Jinx said. "It's almost exactly the same situation as you guys!"

Maybe the ghost had coasted on the memories of better times, she thought. *Until the brothers disrupted that.*

Devon said, slowly, "And that's why we heard 'listen.'" He looked at Todd. "John was trying to get me to listen to you. Like he didn't listen to his brother." He smiled at Todd. "And I am listening. I promise. When daylight hits, we're going to a treatment program."

Todd slapped him on the shoulder. "I'll be right by your side."

A slight breeze came from nowhere Jackson could think of and moved around the room. Suddenly he felt peaceful and light. He felt good. Looking at the others, he knew they felt the same.

"I think John approves," Jackson said.

C H A P T E R 14

"So, you never got to use your banishing stones, huh?" Jinx snapped off the end of her Twizzler with her teeth and cuddled into her couch. *Ghost Hunters* played on the TV, and Jackson stared at the episode intently.

"What?" he said.

"Gah, Jackson, are you that bored? We've seen this episode a million times."

He turned to her. "Yeah, it's just I never paid much attention before to the techniques they use, trying to get a ghost to manifest.

It's, um, fascinating stuff."

Jinx's face crumpled up in confusion. "Why would you *want* a ghost to appear? I thought we are trying to get rid of them."

Jackson shrugged. "Anyway, what did you say before?"

Jinx took another bite of her Twizzler. "The banishing stones," she said. "You never got to use them."

Jackson ran his hand through his hair, still half-watching the episode. "Yeah, well, Todd and Devon almost seemed to want to keep their ghost there."

Jinx nodded. "Well, really, the ghost *is* what got them to actually talk instead of fight. And now Devon's in that program . . . I guess the ghost really did help, even if it threw some shot glasses along the way. And I have to admit, the atmosphere in there did feel nice and cozy. Even if John hid your car keys."

Jackson's face went dreamy, and Jinx snapped her fingers in front of his face. "What is going on with you today?"

Jackson seemed to snap back to the present.

He slapped Jinx's hand away and grabbed a Twizzler. He seemed extra happy all of a sudden. Jinx shrugged it off.

She grabbed her laptop. "Jackson, we are going to get so many more page views after I post this stuff from the tavern." *And then Haley won't forget my name*, she thought to herself. *Nobody will.*

"Also, I want to show you these T-shirts I designed." She could sense Jackson's eyes rolling.

"Why do we need T-shirts again?"

She sighed. "We need to be competitive, Jackson," she explained in what she thought of as her most patient voice. "Get our brand out there."

"For what?"

"For money, of course!" Jinx looked at him indignantly. Why else would she be doing this?

Jackson smirked. "Like how we got so much money from Todd?"

Jinx squirmed and shifted her attention back to her computer. "That was different. That was a special circumstance."

"That had nothing to do with the fact that you thought Todd was cute?"

Jinx could feel herself start to blush. "What are you, a girl?" she snapped. "I just couldn't charge him while his brother was going through all that."

Jackson nodded—a little smugly, Jinx thought.

Just then, a ping sounded on her computer—the alert that told her when she got an email from the Paranormalists website. She looked at Jackson. They hadn't had an actual email before. Lots of comments to her blogs, for sure (a few of them for hair-growth products or weight-loss pills from spambots), but never an actual email.

She squealed a little. Even Jackson seemed a little excited.

He leaned over her shoulder as she opened the message.

Dear Paranormalist Investigators:

I'm new in town, and I came across your website. I see you're from Portland. That's good, because I need some help. Some local help.

You see, I'm in danger, and so is my mom. Our house is haunted, and we can't get rid of it. Can you help us? What is your rate?

Sincerely,

Mayhem on Mohawk Ave

Jinx looked at Jackson. She could feel tingles up and down her spine. She smiled huge at him.

"Looks like we have our next case."

SEEK THE TRUTH
AND FIND THE CAUSE
WITH
THE PARANORMALISTS

CASE 1:
THE HAUNTING OF APARTMENT 101

Jinx was a social reject who became a punked-out paranormal investigator. Jackson is a jock by day and Jinx's ghost-hunting partner by night. When a popular girl named Emily asks the duo to explore a haunting in her dad's apartment, Jinx is skeptical—but Jackson insists they take the case. And the truth they find is even stranger than Emily's story.

CASE 2:
THE TERROR OF BLACK EAGLE TAVERN

Jinx's ghost-hunting partner Jackson may be a jock, but Jinx is not interested in helping his football buddy Todd—until Todd's case gets too weird to ignore. A supernatural presence is causing chaos at the bar Todd's family owns. And the threat has a connection to Todd that's deeper than even he realizes . . .

CASE 3:
THE MAYHEM ON MOHAWK AVENUE

Jinx and Jackson have become the go-to ghost hunters at their high school. When a new kid in town tries to get in on their business, Jinx is furious. Portland only needs one team to track down ghosties! But Jinx's quest to shut down her competition will lead her and Jackson down a dangerous path . . .

CASE 4:
THE BRIDGE OF DEATH

Jinx is the top paranormal investigator at her high school, and she has a blog to prove it. Jackson's her ghost-hunting partner by night—former partner, anyway. After a shakeup in the Paranormalists' operation, the two ex-best friends are on the outs, and at the worst possible time. Because a deadly supernatural threat is putting their classmates in harm's way . . .

AFTER THE DUST SETTLED

The world is over.
Can you survive what's next?

Check out NIGHT FALL
for the best in YA horror!

THE
protectors

THAW

Lock-In

The PrAnK

skin

UNTHINKABLE

The COMBINATION

MESSAGES
FROM
BEYOND

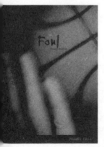

Foul

the club

THE
LATE
BUS

Last DesSerts

MEGAN ATWOOD

lives in Minneapolis, MN, and gets to write books for a living. She also teaches writing classes and reads as many young adult books as she can get her hands on. She only occasionally investigates paranormal activity.